THIS BOOK BELONGS
TO
children's
choice®

Dori Mangarella

# *Noisy Nora*

Story and pictures by Rosemary Wells

The Dial Press · New York

 · Library of Congress Catalog Card Number: 72-7599 · Printed in the United States of America
Sixth Printing, 1979
Designed by Jane Byers Bierhorst
ISBN: 0-590-75802-0

for Joan Read

Jack had dinner early,

Father played with Kate,

Jack needed burping,

So Nora had to wait.

First she banged the window,

Then she slammed the door,

Then she dropped her sister's marbles
on the kitchen floor.

"Quiet!" said her father.
"Hush!" said her mum.

"Nora!" said her sister,
"Why are you so dumb?"

Jack had gotten filthy,

Mother cooked with Kate,

Jack needed drying off,

So Nora had to wait.

First she knocked the lamp down,

Then she felled some chairs,

Then she took her brother's kite

And flew it down the stairs.

"Quiet!" said her father.
"Hush!" said her mum.

"Nora!" said her sister,
"Why are you so dumb?"

Jack was getting sleepy,

Father read with Kate,

Jack needed singing to,

So Nora had to wait.

"I'm leaving!" shouted Nora,
"And I'm never coming back!"

And they didn't hear a sound
But a tralala from Jack.

Father stopped his reading.
Mother stopped her song.

"Mercy!" said her sister,
"Something's very wrong."

No Nora in the cellar.
No Nora in the tub.

No Nora in the mailbox
Or hiding in a shrub.

"She's left us!" moaned her mother

As they sifted through the trash.

"But I'm back again!" said Nora
With a monumental crash.

# Look Who's Part of the Children's Choice® Family!

## Something special for Children's Choice® Book Club members

You can get all these storybook favorites—Puss in Boots, Babar, Curious George, Lyle, George and Martha and The Year at Maple Hill Farm—to hang up on your wall. They're big (17″ × 22″) and beautiful posters, printed in full color on high quality paper. Best of all, you can get all 6 for just $3.95, including postage and handling.

To order your set of 6 Children's Choice® posters, please send your name, address and $3.95 in check or money order to:

**CHILDREN'S CHOICE® POSTERS**
**2931 East McCarty St.**
**P.O. Box 1068**
**Jefferson City, Mo. 65102**

Please allow 3-6 weeks for delivery. Your posters are mailed in a tube, so they won't be creased at all.

Offer expires December 31, 1980